THE
MYSTERIOUS DISAPPEARANCE
AT BIRD BRIDGE

THE
MYSTERIOUS
DISAPPEARANCE
AT
BIRD BRIDGE

A DOG DETECTIVE STORY

VIV LEVY

Gothic Image
PUBLICATIONS

First Edition published in hardback in 2013 by
Gothic Image Publications,
7 High Street, Glastonbury,
Somerset BA6 9DP England.

www.gothicimage.co.uk

ISBN 978 0 906362 75 4

A CIP catalogue record for this book is
available from the British Library

Design and text styling by Bernard Chandler, Glastonbury
Text set in Univers Medium 12/18pt

Printed and bound in Malta by Gutenberg Press

DEDICATION
And Acknowledgements

This book is dedicated to Clare Allan, Elsie's person. Their company on Heath walks inspired this story as we fantasised about the mischief Dot and Elsie were likely to get up to. Clare contributed to some of the writing which enabled me to realise this tale.

To Frances Howard-Gordon who had faith in the book and took on the mammoth task of editing and publishing the work.

And, of course, to Dot (aka Sophie) and Elsie for being themselves, for taking us on walks and keeping us smiling.

I would also like to thank Battersea Cats and Dogs Home. Fidel and Flo were my companions for their lives' span and were rehomed from Battersea.

Thank you to Mary and Jasmina who ARE Enfield Dog Rescue. Dot (aka Sophie) was one of the many dogs they bring over from Ireland. I am so grateful for her.

Thanks to Jack and Rose Abraham; they are steadfast friends and Jack is the wonderful vet who has looked after all my dogs.

And thank you Bryan Kneale R.A. for his unstinting encouragement of all my enterprises.

INTRODUCTION

This was probably an unconventional way of creating a book.

The puppies started it. Sophie (aka Dot) and Elsie were four and a half months old when they first met on Hampstead Heath. It was love at first sight and energetic play ensued. Elsie's person, Clare, who was instrumental in the realisation of the story, and I wasted many happy hours just watching them interact. Their antics led to fantasies about the exploits and trouble this mismatched pair might get into. I started drawing them. As the drawings evolved so the story followed, until a symbiotic relationship between images and text emerged. The dogs complied as they met and befriended others on the Heath.

Fidel, Flo and Sophie (aka Dot) are based on my previous companions and, in Sophie's case, on my current friend. All three have been life savers in more ways than one. I am eternally grateful to Battersea Dogs and Cats Home and Enfield Dog Rescue for allowing me to adopt these wonderful dogs.

All similarities to characters, dead or alive, are deliberate although names have sometimes been changed in the interest of the narrative.

I hope that dog lovers of all ages will enjoy and get as many laughs, and some tears, out of this book as I have experienced through living and walking with the protagonists and the people who inspired it.

It is hard to believe that Sophie and Elsie are now five and a half years old. They still meet up and play the same games although they may have acquired some new hobbies along the way. I wonder if they might have another adventure in them.

EVERYTHING YOU CAN IMAGINE IS REAL

Pablo Picasso

PART ONE

PROLOGUE

She walked down the aisle with her tail held high, like a bride on her wedding day. We stood with our noses pressed to the wire; some whined, some barked; she passed graciously, like a queen. We listened as the footsteps faded away, the light clicking of her claws and the harsh clack of the high-heeled shoes beside her. When the door opened she walked through without looking back. The scent of her lingered, grew fainter but the soft early summer scent of her lingered for weeks, for months, a trace of a scent, a trace of a trace, until the desolate morning I woke to find her gone.

THE MEETING ON THE HEATH

Let's pretend that you've never heard of two dogs called Dot and Elsie. It's hard to imagine that there was ever a time when the part of London known as Hampstead Heath didn't resound to their names. So synonymous have their names become with those eight hundred acres of wild grass and woodland, that a London dog travelling anywhere in Britain, on mentioning that he knows the place, is likely to find himself the focus of starstruck attention. I even heard of an incident in Winnipeg.

A Schnauzer, as I understand, recently emigrated and dizzied by the endless plains, happened to mention to a Bichon Frise how heartsick he felt for the hills of Hampstead, the squirrel packed woods, the muddy slopes so marvellous for rolling, when a gasp drew him out of his reverie. "Oh, oh, oh! You know Hampstead Heath! Did you ever see Dot and Elsie?"

The Schnauzer acknowledged that not only had he seen them, he had even played with them and had a ball wrested out of his mouth by an unrepentant Elsie.

"Wow!" cried the Bichon, "did you keep the ball?"

"I never got it back!" and it was clear that the fact still rankled with him.

"What about Dot?" gushed the Bichon, "she's SOOO pretty! Is she as pretty in the flesh?" and the Schnauzer had to admit that she was.

At four months old Dot and her two sisters were shipped to a dog rescue centre in London. From there she was adopted and walked every day on Hampstead Heath. It was on the Heath that she met tiny four-month-old Elsie, the smallest Staffie in the world. The two of them played and played and, as they grew, went

on progressively ambitious adventures, frequently
getting each other and their people into trouble.
Elsie was a bundle of muscle with a leg at each
corner and an irresistible smile. She had a unique
vocal range which she employed to ear-splitting
effect when she required attention. Her tail exuded
confidence and a proud sense of entitlement.
In spite of her small size everything about her
was larger than life. Dot, in contrast, had a dancer's
physique. She could jump and twirl and run like a
gazelle. She rarely barked, preferring to vocalise

through her tail which, depending on
her mood, would curl into a perfect
circle over her back or reverse into a
line of beauty towards the ground.
Her enormous ears played an
important supporting role; they would
stand out at right angles to her head
in seduction mode or pin themselves
back in disapproval or fear; they
would even move independently of
each other when she was puzzled.

She trotted like a dressage horse and could take corners at speed which enabled her to outrun larger dogs and was a source of frustration to Elsie who was a world class sprinter as long as she was travelling in a straight line. They were an unlikely pair.

Dot and Elsie's rise to stardom came about largely as a result of greed. There are people on the Heath who walk around with pockets full of treats. Our two heroines were adept at sniffing out the purveyors of goodies and the queen of eats was the old lady who kept a bag of homemade liver cake for her Battersea dog Fidel. She would generously hand over squares of cake from her usual bench at the east end of Bird Bridge. Imagine Dot and Elsie's shock when, one morning, they found their friend sitting there in despair, so upset that she forgot to dispense their favourite treats! Fidel has disappeared; she doesn't know what to do and couldn't face making liver cake today. She tells them of her fear that Fidel has been stolen to be used as bait by a dog-fighting ring, or that he might be held to ransom, which she would not be able to pay as she lived on a very small pension.

Dot and Elsie listened as intently as they could to her story and found themselves irretrievably drawn in, a most unusual occurrence in such spontaneous creatures. Elsie began to whimper hysterically, and then became gripped by anger, then rage:

"We must go on a Quest, for the sake of all dog-fight victims...and the best liver cake in the world."

Notices sprang up on trees and lampposts appealing for sightings of Fidel. His Identikit picture, put together by the police from a catalogue of canine features,

10

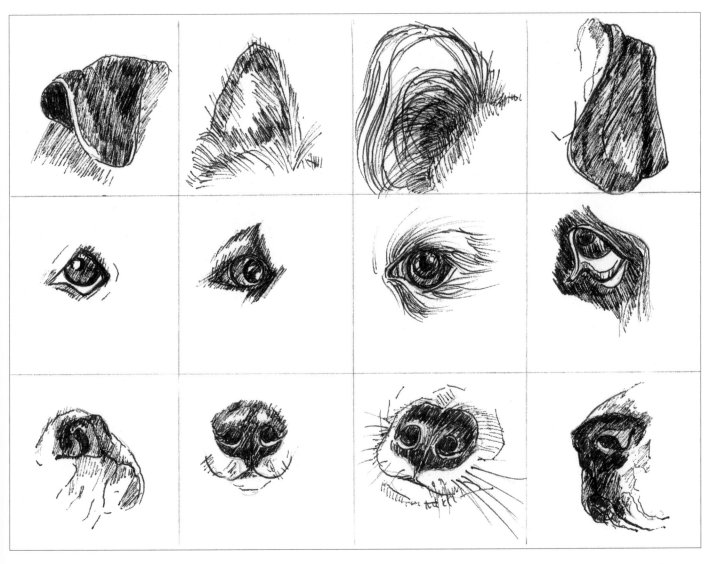

was, to say the least, peculiar and extremely unflattering. The old lady had no photos of Fidel and had been too distressed and confused to describe her companion accurately. She almost forgot what he looked like. "Typical London hairy" was the best she could come up with.

Although Dot and Elsie could make neither head nor tail of the posted images, they knew exactly what Fidel looked and smelled like, a bit like liver cake, and resolved to find him. They had heard of Bloodhounds who tracked down criminals and had witnessed police dogs going about their business; they didn't seem to be making much headway in this case, had no leads, although they were firmly attached to their handlers by mighty chain ones. They knew about search and rescue dogs. How hard could it be? With Dot's sighthound genes and Elsie's inquisitive nose they were bound to triumph where all others failed.

Brimming with confidence, they immediately embarked on a disorganised to-ing and fro-ing, treating the whole enterprise like an elaborate game. They rummaged in the undergrowth and dug holes in a frantic search for clues; they gazed into puddles and ponds only to be confronted by reflections of their own, astonished expressions. Tired and demoralised, they paused long enough to formulate a strategy and started dog-to-dog enquiries. At first they were met with aggression and indifference but they persevered and, eventually, came up with a lead.

THE QUEST BEGINS

Gossip was an obese Labrador. She really was enormously fat, cranky and bitter. She was so fat she was barely recognisable as a Labrador, her face was swamped by blubber, she was so huge it was all she could do to sway from the car park to the café accompanied by her overweight person who would bag a table, slump down gasping for breath after the painfully short lumber from the car, and would remain installed there for the day consuming large helpings of breakfast, lunch, afternoon tea and cake. Gossip fancied herself as the fount of all knowledge and would hold court, jealously guarded by JR, an outsize vicious and evil-tempered Jack Russell.

The two of them hung around begging for scraps and stealing entire cooked breakfasts when the opportunity arose.

Dot and Elsie were not averse to the odd scrap or two from the café tables so they set off quite happily for Kenwood. Little did they know what lay in store for them at the paws of Gossip and her sidekick. They spotted the fount of all knowledge slumped in her usual spot and ran straight up to her, ignoring the tantalising smells coming from the full English breakfasts being enjoyed by early punters. JR, who sat concealed behind Gossips' enormous rolls of fat, pounced, hackles up, teeth bared, swearing and shouting. The girls nearly jumped out of their fur and retreated to a safe distance, having almost forgotten the speech they had carefully rehearsed en route.

"We're really, really sorry. We didn't mean to disturb you and we haven't eaten any of your treats. We only wanted to ask you one question. What happened to Fidel and how can we find him?"

"That's two questions," snarled gossip.

"Well, it's only one question each," reasoned Elsie as a trembling Dot prayed that matters had not been made worse by Elsie's cheek.

Gossip seemed to swell to twice her huge size causing Dot to quake in fear while Elsie remained blissfully unaware of the ice-cold atmosphere and the row of poisonous yellow teeth that JR was baring prior to a full-on assault. A timely sausage, lobbed from a nearby table, intervened. JR pounced and returned to share the prize with Gossip who inhaled the morsel at speed before returning her attention to her young petitioners.

"Bring me the head of Dogo Argentino," she growled, "and I may point you in the right direction to find Fidel."

"Who is Dogo Argentino and how can we find HIM?" stammered the girls. JR sniggered.

"You will have to go on a night walk to find him and, believe me, you will know him when you see him. You will have to follow a scent path, his scent is 'Wee no.9', frightfully common but popular among the less discerning brutes of his generation."

Dot and Elsie had met dogs of all shapes, sizes and breeds over the course of their sojourns on the Heath.

19

23

They had met German Shepherds, Hungarian Vislas and Pulis, American Mastiffs, Australian Kelpies, Irish Terriers, Scotties and Welsh Collies. They had made friends with an Egyptian Desert dog who had somehow flown here without wings, unlike the swans they saw flapping over the Hampstead ponds whose ability to fly they envied. They had heard tell of a Leonberger, which Elsie was convinced was something you could eat, until she was told that it was an enormous dog bred to resemble a lion and that attempting to eat it was a very bad idea indeed. They had been intimidated by packs of Huskies and cowed by Rhodesian Ridgebacks, baffled by an African Basenji who couldn't bark and perplexed by a hairless dog that hailed from Mexico.

They had been terrified by Oberman Doberman who looked surreal with his cropped ears, stump of a tail, his mighty spiked collar as well as a cruel pinch collar attached to a heavy chain lead, but they had never encountered a Dogo Argentino.

They had played with Shnoodles (Schnauzer/Poodle) and Shnuggles (Schnauzer/Pug), Puggles (Poodle/Pug), Cockerpoos (Cocker Spaniel/Poodle), Goldendoodles (Golden Retriever/Poodle) and a Labradoodle (Labrador/Poodle) who claimed to be a descendant of Greyfriars Bobby.

People frequently asked what Dot was, the usual answer being: "she's a dog" or occasionally "she's a Jacket" (Jack Russell/Whippet). Dot wasn't too happy about this as she knew that a jacket was an inanimate object that a person threw on to indicate WALK; she knew of a disgruntled Collie Springer Spaniel cross called Annie who was referred to as a Sprolly, surely related to a brolly, which was a sort of roof on a stick and was an early warning of an outing in the rain and the humiliating possibility of being dressed in a mac.

Elsie was quite proud of her mac which was bright yellow with a red lining and a hood; it made her look like an intrepid lifeboat dog.

"I've just heard about a dog called Spike," said Dot, "his person says he's a Collidor. Can you believe it?"

"Don't be ridiculous," replied an incredulous Elsie, "what he actually said is that Spike sits in the corridor to guard the front door."

"You don't get it, do you Elsie: they call me a Jacket because I'm a Jack Russell/Whippet, Annie is a Sprolly because she's a Springer Spaniel/Collie, not an umbrella, and Spike is a Collidor because he's Collie/Labrador and nothing to do with a corridor or a front door. You're so full of yourself, Elsie, because you think you're the only proper dog in the world, Staffie/Staffie/Staffie..." And with that Dot pranced off before a furious Elsie could barrel into her. It really was a stupid row as dogs are just dogs and not responsible for their parentage. But the two girls were secretly beginning to wonder whether they had taken on an impossible challenge and could not help venting their frustrations on each other.

The only fact that Dot and Elsie knew to be true was that Dogo Argentino was a foreigner, a Chihuahua perhaps, who would not present much of a problem as there were two of them and only one very small one of it.

The two friends were apprehensive to say the least but there was no alternative, no other lines of enquiry to pursue. Dot and Elsie sloped off to plan a night expedition. Although they had never been out on the Heath in the dark before, they were determined to be brave and to succeed on the first leg of their quest.

ENCOUNTER WITH DOGO

The next night, after the last official walk with their humans, Dot and Elsie managed to slip away and set off, with some trepidation, for a meeting with "THE Dogo", whoever he turned out to be. They were acutely aware of being scrutinized by a multitude of predatory eyes as they strained to keep to the path that had been scented out for them.

Suddenly there was a deafening crash as, out of the gloom, an enormous white shape emerged. The gargantuan head housed a spectacular jaw studded with a trillion terrifying teeth, a paw could have crushed Dot's delicate skull with just one swipe, muscle rippled over his deep chest... Oh no, THIS was Dogo Argentino, no chihuahua he! The girls trembled and quaked as the ghostly apparition headed towards them and slowly lowered itself down to their eye level.

34

A deep and surprisingly mellow voice issued from the head that they had been ordered to get for Gossip.

"What can I do for you two?" he asked in a surprisingly unthreatening tone of growl.

"Um, um, ahhh, well... this is frightfully embarrassing..." managed Dot, who was still recovering from the shock of encountering the biggest dog she had ever seen manifest out of the night. Elsie, the less inhibited of the two, decided to come straight out with it.

"We have to get your head for Gossip in order for her to tell us where to look for the old lady's lost dog, Fidel, so

that we can reunite them and get liver cake and the recipe and be famous and you're so enormous I really don't see how we're supposed to manage it...." She blurted this out at great speed to get it over with before her courage failed.

Dogo made a sound that they hoped was benign and said: "I suspect you misunderstood the mission unless Gossip was being extra mean. You see the two of us have had our portraits painted by Gnasher Freud, he of the cruel and truthful eye, and Gossip said he made her look fat! In my opinion she would have been better off going to grandfather Freud for a diagnosis, but all is vanity and greed with that one. I can't imagine what mischief she had in mind when she set you this challenge; all I know is that she was insanely jealous of my portrait, an excellent likeness and much admired. My advice, if there is no alternative route to the information you need, is go back and get old misery guts to clarify the task she set you."

The girls made their way home, less afraid now, but not looking forward to their next meeting with Gossip who had turned out to be far more terrifying than the gentle giant Dogo.

Dot and Elsie endured a disturbed night of dreams and nightmares. They dreamt of glory and fame, of their reception when they returned with Fidel. Elsie dreamt of sprouting wings, of flying over the Heath, of swooping down over crowds of admirers. She dreamt of liver cake, steak, chicken and marrow bones. Dot was plagued by nightmares: terrifying encounters with Gossip, shredded by JR and eaten with fried egg and chips by the ever expanding Labrador, or squashed, trapped forever beneath her impossible rolls of fat. The two dogs ran and yelped in their sleep, their eyes rolled, their noses twitched and their humans were repeatedly woken with plans for a visit to the vet in the morning before putting the interruptions down to indigestion and turning back to sleep. At last day dawned and reality seemed infinitely worse than nightmares.

Dot and Elsie were less enthusiastic than usual about their daily trip to the Heath. They were exhausted after the night's excursion and they were not used to planning expeditions into the unknown, usually playing things by ear and nose and relying on instinct to lead them to fun and keep them out of danger. Today they would have to angle proceedings towards the Kenwood café and suffer the wrath of Gossip while dodging JR's teeth.

"This is a grave situation, Elsie, we'd better try to get it right this time," whimpered Dot.

IN TROUBLE AGAIN

Dot and Elsie were not known for their powers of concentration so it was inevitable that they would become distracted from their path to the café and the dreaded re-encounter with Gossip. The distraction came in the form of a speeding tennis ball; the temptation to chase was irresistible; Dot managed to capture it and rush off before the rightful owner could claim it. She and Elsie then proceeded to run around and play with the ball shredding it in the process.

Faye, a smooth-coated blue merle Collie, was known as the good fairy but once aroused her temper was not to be trifled with. Incandescent with rage, she regarded the two juvenile thieves and decided they had to be taught a lesson.

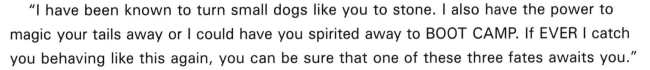

Faye was blessed with one blue and one brown eye, thereby giving her an otherworldly appearance. She stood stock-still, hackles raised, and stared down the miscreants who stopped in their tracks, hypnotised by the strange and unwavering stare. Once she was sure she had their full attention Faye shrieked at them:

"I have been known to turn small dogs like you to stone. I also have the power to magic your tails away or I could have you spirited away to BOOT CAMP. If EVER I catch you behaving like this again, you can be sure that one of these three fates awaits you."

44

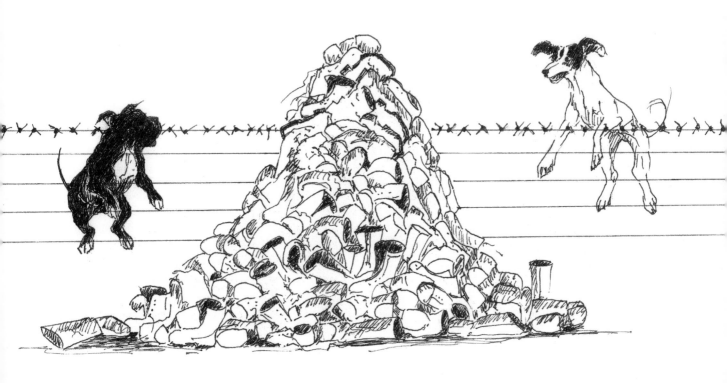

48

49

"Sorry, sorry, really sorry. We won't do it again, promise!" The girls couldn't get over their bad luck as they relinquished the now destroyed ball; they were only having a bit of harmless fun after all.

With their still extant tails between their legs Dot and Elsie sloped off, determined to stay focussed on the task ahead when, as luck would have it, a squeaky ball was flung past them and once again enthusiasm overcame resolution and they were off in pursuit. Unfortunately for them Faye was watching and was still smarting from the theft and destruction of her ball.

"Beware the wrath of COLLIE," she yelled, "be afraid, be very afraid!"

"Guess what," said a trembling Dot, "I think she really can change dogs to stone and cause tails to vanish. Don't you remember the stone dogs we saw on walks in the cemetery? And, come to think of it, we see loads of dogs out here with no tails, dogs whose tails have been cut off."

Carefully they check that their tails are still there.

"You're right," said Elsie, "those poor dogs. Faye must be kept very busy policing ball snatchers! I suppose we should keep a close check on our tails, and hope we don't end up as stone foot-rests in the cemetery. I've never heard of a camp for boots. I suppose we would be forced to eat nothing but boots. I haven't chewed one since I was a puppy. It was tough and not very tasty and I got told off so I really don't fancy ending up in one."

Fraught with anxiety, Dot and Elsie apologised once more. Faye raised a sceptical ear then slowly relented and true to her normal kindly self, forgave them.

The relieved duo now found themselves basking in her magical aura and, much chastened, set off again to the dreaded second interview with Gossip.

Gossip and JR were planted in their usual spot, sniffing the air for signs of stray brunch. They were not pleased to see our two heroines approaching instead of a morsel or three of comforting grub. Gossip was not impressed by the lack of any sign of a dismembered Dogo.

"He was SO big," they stammered, "he said we must have misunderstood you, your magnificence, that his head was going to remain firmly attached to the rest of him...err, ma'am."

"You little idiots, you useless objects, you insignificant upstarts," sneered Gossip "I meant you to destroy the portrait of him. You'll find it in his house, the wee scent will take you there."

Dot and Elsie exchange puzzled glances; Dogo was right, but no one is fatter than Gossip so why does she think she isn't? How could she be so resentful of another's image that she needed to destroy it? They would have to recruit Dogo to their cause and hope that he wouldn't mind a small rearrangement of his portrait.

In the wake of Gossip's splenetic outburst Dot was losing confidence in the success of their mission.

"Do you really think we are useless objects, Else?" she whimpered.

"Of course not, you speak for yourself Dot, I know we are terrifically important and clever and that we are definitely going to find Fidel and become famous and useful and everything, so nose up, liver cake beckons!"

Dot, only mildly reassured, reluctantly agreed to carry on and braced herself for the next stage of their adventure.

That evening Dot and Elsie slipped off again to follow the wee trail to Dogo's house. They were led all the way to Highgate on the north side of the Heath. They sniffed around the Village and down a maze of side streets until they came to a very noisy front door. They could hear Dogo doing a fair imitation of an incensed guard dog and finally managed to make themselves heard over the growling, cursing and door battering coming from inside.

"It's only us, Dot and Elsie, please let us in!"

"I can't open the door, you'll have to come in through the cat flap, try not to terrify the cat!"

Dot had no trouble slipping through the tiny entrance but Elsie, poor Elsie, got stuck halfway through. It was now up to Dot to explain their mission while Elsie let out a series of pitiful shrieks from the cat flap.

"You were right, Dogo, Gossip wants your portrait destroyed. She says she will point us in the direction of lost Fidel if we bring her evidence of your downfall. Please will you join us on our mission?"

"I wouldn't trust Gossip any further than I could throw her, if she was throwable. She's just an inflated bag of poo, but I don't care a woof about the portrait, so why don't we tear a strip off it and get this over with. It's up on the wall in the next room, I am tall enough to reach it so wait there for a morsel of me."

It wasn't long before Dogo was back with a strip of the painting, torn off right through the centre of his noble head.

"This should do the trick. Now you'd better get out of here before the people come home and ruin everything. We will have to heave Elsie out somehow as she does seem to be terminally jammed!"

Between them they pushed and shoved at Elsie until both she and the cat flap took leave of their moorings and Elsie, unable to free herself, clattered and banged down the street, much to the amusement of the watching cat.

Finally Elsie's puzzled human managed to disengage the humiliated creature when she hauled her in for the night. The cause of this latest mishap remained a mystery and a source of much speculation and hilarious stories amongst Heath regulars. Elsie hoped that this sorry tale would not reach the fat, smirking Gossip, who would undoubtedly derive great pleasure and much mileage from it and make vicious fun of her (Elsie's) muscular girth.

So it was that, after a great game of tug with the precious strip of canvas, Dot was dispatched to the café to present the bribe.

"Got it, we've got it! Now will you tell us where to look for Fidel?"

Gossip, planted like a coconut in her usual spot, shifted her weight to peer down at Dot. She seemed singularly unimpressed and would have preferred a large contribution of blood pudding to the grimy shred of canvas that Dot was flapping in her face. She was bored and hungry and decided that anything to get rid of this annoying little dog was worth a try.

"Look towards France," she said, "that's all I'm prepared to tell you."

FRANCE

For Dot and Elsie Hampstead Heath constituted the WORLD.

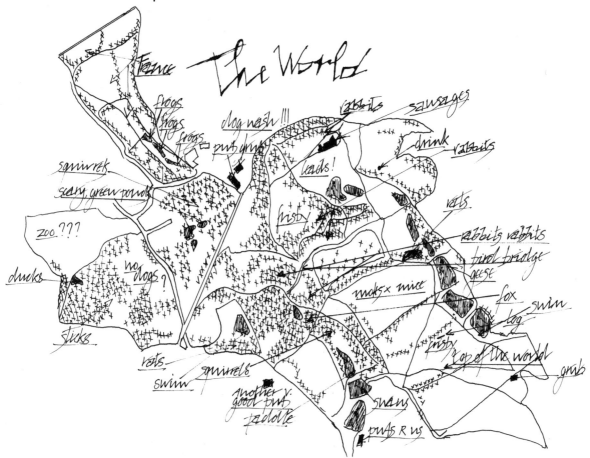

They weren't too sure whether France was a place or something edible but given Gossip's addiction to food, they leaned towards the grocery option. After much deliberation the puzzled dogs decided to do the sensible thing for once and consult Faye. Faye's magical powers were sure to be able to untangle this conundrum. They set off for Parliament Hill, steadfastly ignoring all the tempting tennis balls and Frisbees that were being flung around for their carefree friends.

"Wait a minute," yelped Elsie, "you know huge and hairy Ralf? He claims to be a Bouvier de Flandres, says his ancestors hail from Beglum, or something, and some of them from France. He should know how to get there, we should ask him."

"Good one Else. There's only one problem, we don't know his wee number and we haven't seen him for ages. Unless we run into him soon we're done for. I think we should stick to plan A and trust to Faye."

"Bark, bark, bark, bark, bark, bark, bark, bark..."

"Oh, no, here comes tourettes Daphne to muddle things up. She always has a lot to shout about but keeps repeating herself: biscuit, biscuit, biscuit, biscuit ad infinitum. I agree wholeheartedly with biscuits but I'd much rather eat them than advertise them. She's no help at all to two hard-pushed detectives with more important matters on their minds," moaned an outraged Elsie.

The two dogs had been steadfast in their resolve to eschew the missiles being retrieved by their mates, but they were doomed to be distracted by eccentrics, biscuits, and shortlived alternative plans. It was time to get back on track and find Faye, but the girls were out of sorts. Elsie was visibly wilting. How long was she going to be able to

63

carry on without the promise of sustenance? It was only the hovering mirage of trays of scrumptious liver cake, just out of reach, that kept her from fainting right away. Dot was being uncharacteristically snappy, wanting nothing to do with potential admirers or offers of play. The longed for smell of success and liver had to be within nose reach.

Faye was sitting at the top of the hill, contemplating the view and looking out for miscreants. She stood and wagged her tail as the girls approached. They took this as a good sign and ran up to her bursting with questions, anticipating an instant solution to their quest.

"Faye, Faye you've got to help us. Gossip says look towards France. What is it? Can you eat it? Where is it?"

"Slow down. I can help you but there is no point in rushing around like tripe hounds. OK. France is a place. A place in the world. Rude people sometimes call the inhabitants of this place 'frogs'. This is because they eat frogs' legs, not a dish I would recommend. Even Gossip might find it unpalatable."

"Where in the world?" chorused the impatient duo.

"Hold on. I must have time to think and sniff the wind."

And sitting back down on the top of the highest hill in London, Faye raised her long aristocratic nose and inhaled the breeze, slowly turning her head to all points of the compass. She concentrated on summoning up images from her past for she had been born and brought up in Glastonbury until her people had moved to London to open a bookshop. Before the move to London, which she had heard was a very scary place, Faye had spent hours in front of a mirror trying to re-educate her expression. She had tried to transform her otherworldly face into a snarling, angry mask. The new look had stood her in good stead on several occasions. She had, for instance, managed to drum some manners into the likes of Dot and Elsie, but now she realised that working against her true nature and the powers invested in her in a former life was a backward step.

'Give me a puppy before the age of twelve weeks and I will give you the dog' was a truism that was hard to ignore. She had to acknowledge, however, that 'teaching an old dog new tricks' was possible and, sometimes, necessary. She recalled her early puppyhood and fond memories of the Tor, ceremonies on another hill, where she gained her reputation as a white witch.

Nostalgia overwhelmed her. In Glastonbury she was unique, she turned heads whenever she sailed down the High Street. In Glastonbury she was a Guardian. In Glastonbury her powers were recognised and she was treated with due respect. Nobody there would have dared to destroy her ball, the one that enabled her to project into the future. Faye realised that Dot and Elsie understood her powers and that this was a perfect opportunity to establish her reputation and to work good magic on the Heath. She shook herself out of her reverie and concentrated on retrieving the scent of France.

"I think I've got it, a distinct waft of frogs coming from over there. You must be careful as you will have to cross two busy roads on the way. Beware of red herrings en route! Now I have to be off. Collies are working dogs and I have a lot of jobs to catch up on."

With that Faye wagged a goodbye and galloped off down the hill.

Dot and Elsie were now one step forward but wondered what on earth a red herring could be. Was there to be no end to the obstacles inhibiting a successful conclusion to their search?

As it happened the girls were about to find out about red herrings.

Dot stuck her nose down holes in the hope of a whiff of France while Elsie rolled in the delicious summer grasses.

Then Dot spotted a true aristocrat, a beautiful lurcher, known as Araminta Woodgush, and couldn't resist rushing up to her to discover where she had found her splendid, jewel encrusted collar.

Araminta blinked her enormous, khol-lined eyes and thought back to her vast collection of collars and coats: "I seem to remember that my person brought this one back from France.

France is the Mecca of high fashion and this collar is a limited edition Maison TouTou. My person sometimes borrows it to wear on special occasions."

Dot, overcome with envy, momentarily forgot the reason for their mission and became even more determined to find France. She turned to Elsie, who was blissfully rolling in an unspeakable smell, and exhorted her to "GET A GRIP" and hurry up before all the collars sell out! "Honestly, Elsie, sometimes you don't know which way up you are."

"Keep your fur on," growled Elsie, "I must make sure that I have rubbed enough of this delicious perfume behind my ears."

Having satisfied their vanity, they pulled themselves together and started investigating the water holes and ponds that described a route across the Heath. At last, they came to the first main road. Spaniards Road was a fast and terrifying crossing. They didn't know how best to negotiate it, they had been taught to never cross unaccompanied and decided to wait for someone to lead them to the other side.

Eventually and very luckily Dogo appeared on a lead with his person so they attached themselves to him and arrived safely, conga style, onto sandy Heath. It was dark and hilly here and they thought for one glorious moment that they had spotted Fidel racing across the brow of a tree-lined mound. He was there and then he was gone in the direction of the second road.

By the time the girls reached Wildwood Road there was no sign of dog or man, just the dark wood behind them and another stretch of unexplored land in front. They were impatient by now and, instead of waiting at the kerb, they made a mad dash across the road where they were narrowly missed by a blaring 4x4. It took them some time to recover their senses and to stop trembling before looking around them and wondering yet again if they had arrived in France.

Tentatively they crept forward following a strange scent that meandered into marshy undergrowth and pricked their ears to the strangest sounds they had ever heard. There was a pop and then something, a small slimy something, with unusually long back legs, propelled itself out of the bog and stared up at the two astonished dogs. Several other croaking, hopping creatures closely followed it.

"FROGS!" yelped Elsie.
"This must be France!" sighed Dot.

At last, the seekers knew they were near the end of their search.

PART TWO

FIDEL

Fidel and Flo were brother and sister. They were strays, born on a London rubbish dump. Their mother had been run over and the siblings were left to survive on their own. Fidel quickly learnt to scavenge in the bins outside big houses and supermarkets; he shared his spoils with his sister and was adept at finding warm places to sleep in abandoned boxes and by central heating vents. He had a thick, dark, rough coat to keep him warm and flourished on filthy scraps, whereas Flo was an elegant, wispy blond who was, in her opinion, clearly meant for better things. She was not thriving on the street and Fidel knew that something radical would have to be done if she was to survive.

One cold morning, as they were gloomily trailing around the streets, rummaging in the garbage dumped outside restaurants, they were brought up short by an imposing Staffordshire bull terrier called Socrates. He was tied to a bus stop waiting for his person to emerge from a café with breakfast.

"You poor things," he said, "you look cold and hungry. Is there anything I can do to help?"

"Maybe," answered Fidel, "I really need to get my sister off the street, she isn't cut out for this life, and you can see how fragile she is. Have you any ideas?"

"I found my person at Battersea Dog's Home and he changed my name from

Gnasher to Socrates, quite appropriate, apart from the fact that he calls me Sock for short. The indignity of it. Anyway, he means well and I suggest you go along there and turn yourselves in. Although it's very noisy, you will get bed and board. If you're lucky you will be able to adopt a person and find a good home in no time at all. The people there love us all and will teach you how to seduce a potential friend as soon as possible, although I don't think your sister will have a problem in that department, she really is very pretty."

There was no alternative. Fidel remembered the building at the southeast end of Battersea Park, he remembered hearing the barking and wondering what went on inside. Now that he knew asylum lay beyond those walls, he made up his mind to take the advice and set off with Flo to seek refuge.

There were already two dogs tied to the gates outside the home looking confused and anxious, their tails firmly tucked between their legs. Just as Fidel was having second thoughts, the gates opened and they were all welcomed in.

They were ushered in to meet the VET. This was a first for Flo and Fidel who had never been subjected to a medical checkup. The vet was really very kind. He crouched down to stroke and to speak. He spoke Dog to the two dishevelled vagrants before checking them for parasites, taking their temperatures and examining their teeth to try and assess their age. When he was satisfied with his inspection he injected them and treated them for fleas. They were too disorientated to object and delighted when they were offered treats before being led off to the kennels. There they were separated for the first time in their lives as dogs and bitches were kept apart.

They were fed and given beds. Flo was so exhausted she immediately fell asleep but Fidel was overcome with anxiety and spent the rest of the day craning his head between the bars of his kennel trying to keep an eye on Flo who was housed across the way.

For two weeks the two dogs were vetted for health and temperament until they were deemed fit for rehoming. Then Fidel and Flo were led out to meet potential adopters. Having never lived in a home before, the two strays didn't know how best to behave. Fidel was suspicious and uncommunicative whereas Flo's beauty ensured that she was swiftly snapped up. Fidel watched with mixed feelings as Flo was taken out of her kennel, fitted with a collar and lead and walked off without him.

He stood with his nose pressed to the wire; he whined and sometimes barked as Flo walked down the aisle with her nose in the air like a bride on her wedding day. She walked out of the door without looking back. He listened as the footsteps disappeared, the delicate tack tack tack of her claws and the clack of the heels beside her. The scent of his sister lingered, a trace of a scent, a trace of a trace, until that desolate morning when he woke to find her gone.

As time went by Fidel fretted and pined for his sister. The carers at the home became more and more concerned as this loyal hound lost weight and seemed increasingly demoralised as he was overlooked by the public.

An old lady arrived one day and stopped by Fidel's kennel. She remained there transfixed by the sad face that refused to respond to her overtures. He reminded her of her own lonely plight. She crouched down to his level and tentatively offered

a square of her homemade liver cake. Fidel's nose twitched. This was a new, irresistible smell. He bellycrawled towards the morsel and, eventually, accepted it. He took another piece and another until his tail began to wag and he got to his feet and licked the hand that fed him. Although the old lady had imagined adopting a smaller companion, and had really wanted a girl, she found herself in love with this sad handsome boy and hurried to sign him into her care.

Fidel went with the old lady all the way to Kilburn where she lived in a modest but comfortable flat. She took him shopping to buy a bed, although he would end up sleeping with her; she bought dog food and biscuits, although he would end up sharing her meals and she bought liver in order to make a large supply of his favourite treat. Fidel had fallen on his paws; the only thing that worried him was the whereabouts of his sister.

Every morning Fidel and the old lady would head off for Hampstead Heath where they would walk for hours and sit awhile on their favourite bench at the east side of Bird Bridge. It was here that they first encountered Dot and Elsie, who were experts at divining the contents of pockets. They could detect liver cake at a hundred paces and would head off for Bird Bridge at the first opportunity. The gentle and indulgent Fidel would look on as his supplies were dispensed to the two over-excited girls.

The old lady, who rarely changed her routine, had read of a dog show to be held one Sunday in Hyde Park. She decided to take Fidel along. He was after all the most beautiful dog in the world and deserved to have his beauty officially recognised. She couldn't have guessed what the consequences of her decision would be.

THE DOG SHOW

Stalls surrounded the showground selling an astonishing array of collars, leads and halters including devices to stop pulling, stop barking, biting and scratching. There were stalls offering sinister looking rakes, combs and vicious steel brushes, vile smelling shampoos and unguents, every imaginable product to make a dog appear more human than dog. There was even coloured varnish for claws, stick-on earrings and clothes for pampered pets, including woolly hats, knitted jumpers and fur-lined raincoats with some sporting hoods. The old lady couldn't resist spending some of her scarce income on a splendid padded leather collar to complement Fidel's tweedy shaggy coat.

There were stalls selling toys and stalls selling gourmet treats, including doggy ice cream and cakes although none as tasty as the famous secret liver cake. How Dot and Elsie would have loved these food stalls but they, alas, had other red herrings to fry. There was a registration tent where dogs could be entered for various classes. Prettiest bitch, most handsome dog, waggiest tail, best six legs, most original costume were just some of the competitions. The place heaved with fairies, batdogs, busybees, dogs dressed as police people, fire people and debutantes in evening dress.

It was a surreal scene as the costumed dogs mingled with dogs just being dogs. Fidel was mystified by the spectacle of dogs in clothes, let alone these bizarre costumes, and the old lady looked in vain for a class offering a reward for the fittest dog, a prize that her boy would surely have carried off. There was, of course, the grand finale Best in Show where competition reached fever pitch and people cast daggers at their rivals.

Amidst the chaos and confusion, the sweaty smells from armpits and hamburger stalls, Fidel's gaze alighted on a blond mixed breed sporting a diamanté collar and lead set. She was being dragged around behind a white standard French Poodle who appeared to be wearing curlers in her topknot and an outrageous confection around her neck. The little blond looked miserable as she was pulled along, her tail firmly tucked between her legs, behind her aristocratic companion.

The more Fidel looked and sniffed the more convinced he became that he had found Flo. As the unhappy blond vanished in the crowd, Fidel started trembling. His tail up, he pulled and panted and suddenly lunged, yanking the lead out of the old lady's hand.

Weaving wildly through the crowd, he barked for Flo. He caught glimpses of the Poodle's topknot and headed towards it until he came to a judging ring. Flo was slumped on the grass while the poodle was having her ridiculous haircut combed out. So as not to alarm her, Fidel crept slowly up to her and whined. She turned her head, uncomprehending at first. She stood, turned, and slowly started wagging her tail as the identity of the large hairy mutt confronting her began to dawn on her. Her tail described wild circles, she wagged her whole body, she licked his nose, she slipped her collar and leapt in the air. Fidel mirrored her joy and the two of them jumped and ran through the crowd, across the park and away.

As soon as they had time to catch their breaths, Fidel was quick to explain that they must find their way back to Hampstead to reassure the old lady who had been so good to him. They daren't go back to find her at the show as Flo was frightened of being recognised and reconnected to her unhappy situation in the poodle household. She would explain everything on their journey back to the Heath. They would have to be careful if they were to avoid dog wardens and well-meaning members of the public who would assume that they were lost.

FLO'S STORY

Flo's relief at being adopted from Battersea was shortlived. It was soon to become clear that the glamorous high-heeled woman who had taken her was after a companion underdog for her show French Poodle. At first Flo had been impressed by the luxurious surroundings of her new home, but playing second fiddle to an arrogant and vain primadonna was to prove a dispiriting, cruel constraint for a young dog who was used to the freedom and love she had experienced with her brother.

The more she weighed up the benefits of a warm, hygienic and fashionable home, set amongst the French themed environs of South Kensington, with the raw, inhospitable streets she roamed with Fidel, the more she understood the superior value of love and the freedom to meet and greet other dogs. Although she had frequently been cold and often hungry, she had never been bored, had never been left on her own for hours in a locked laundry room and chastised for howling her misery to an unheeding world and for chewing the furniture in her frustration, bullied by a large white hairy bitch with ideas above her station. Flo's ambition to star in the homes of the rich had proved to be, at the very least, misguided.

As they wended their way through the back doubles to avoid detection and as Flo's story unfolded, they became irretrievably lost. The wee trails were confusing, as many dogs had walked the streets before them. Fidel kept stopping to sniff the air in the hope of a whiff of the fresh fields of Hampstead Heath but all he received were the fumes of buses and cars. They were stuck in the West End. Flo's paws, unused to padding on concrete, were tender, and her claws, overlong from neglect, were causing her pain. She was walking like a woman whose shoes were too small and too high. They had to stop and rest, they had to find somewhere to sleep for the night. Eventually they curled up together in the dark basement of an empty shop.

They set off again at dawn the next morning. Fidel swore he could smell something vaguely familiar on the air, a feral animal odour, at once reassuring and slightly alarming. At any rate it was far preferable to the disorientating stink of traffic fumes and sweaty humans rushing to work. Fidel decided to follow it. Flo trailed along behind him. She trusted her brother but was, nevertheless, wondering what fate had in store for her this time.

They soon discovered the source of the trail they had been following when they arrived at Regent's Park and found themselves staring into the wolf enclosure at the Zoo. The wolves had never heard of Hampstead Heath and looked quite capable of eating the two wanderers who backed off to the safer manicured areas of the park where they hoped to meet a well-informed dog who would be able to give them directions.

Their next encounter was an English Bull Terrier, sitting like a weather vane, up a tree. This was very strange but surely a dog who could get that far up a tree must be able to see for miles and point them in the right direction!

"Excuse us," shouted Fidel, interrupting the terrier's high-rise meditation, "but can you see the way to Hampstead Heath?"

"I can't see that far," replied the bull terrier, "but I can just make out Primrose Hill, which I think you'll find is well on the way to the Heath. Go up to the top of the hill and you may be able to smell your way from there, or ask one of the local dogs."

Up they went to the top of Primrose Hill. This was clearly a superior class of neighbourhood as Fidel was able to scrounge some very tasty roast beef sandwiches which had been abandoned on a bench; at least he hoped they had been abandoned and that some irate owner wasn't going to suddenly materialise and cause a fuss! He and Flo stuffed down this welcome treat as fast as they could before peering around for a likely guide to the final leg of their journey.

As Faye was on her rounds that morning, she spotted the two strangers, immediately recognising Fidel and guessing where they were heading. She thought of Dot and Elsie and of how excited they would have been to be there and decided not to steal their thunder. So she told Fidel about the search the girls had mounted, told him how worried they were about the old lady and how much they were looking forward to the secret of the liver cake! Fidel of course remembered Dot and Elsie from the Bird Bridge feeding frenzies and was quite happy to go along with Faye's offer of an escort to the top of Parliament Hill, where she would leave them to sniff out the rest of their way unaccompanied. She hoped that they would cross paths with the girls en route.

TWO JOURNEYS END

Now that they had found France, Dot and Elsie knew they were nearing the end of their search. They thought they had spotted Fidel on several occasions but had been misled by his generic London hairy look, and had been embarrassed by nonplussed dogs who vehemently denied that they were Fidel and even had to show their identity tags before Dot and Elsie would admit they were mistaken.

The girls decided to head back to England and Bird Bridge, to inform the old lady of their progress and to maybe, just maybe, be rewarded with some liver cake.

Meanwhile, from their vantage point at the top of Primrose Hill, Fidel and Flo could definitely sense that they were on the right track. They trailed the breeze downhill, along well kept streets, they passed an enormous building called a hospital where lots of people dressed like vets milled around, and then they spotted a miscellany of dogs attached to a human who was being dragged at high speed towards a green horizon. There was a Spaniel with very little behind his nose, there was a Dachshund snaking along on short legs, and what appeared to be a distressed item of soft furnishing lumbering along on baggy paws. There was the tiniest Chihuahua in the world dressed in a ridiculous shocking pink hoody with the word SECURITY stamped in diamanté across the back. This little creature was improbably yoked to a Boxer bodyguard. There was a loping Deerhound concentrating on maintaining a modicum of dignity in the midst of this shambolic pack.

There was a brace of gasping Pugs, their eyes popping with the effort of keeping up and there was a baying Beagle anticipating the freedom of the hunt. Fidel and Flo decided to follow this strange parade and sure enough soon found themselves at the south end of the Heath. As the red-faced human let his charges off their leads, there was an ear-splitting cacophony of barking and swearing as the pack raced off to freedom. The two wanderers distanced themselves from the melée so that Fidel could concentrate on finding his bearings and the way back to Bird Bridge.

As luck would have it Dot and Elsie arrived by the old lady's side at precisely the same time as Fidel and Flo. There was hysteria and joy and liver cake all round. The old lady was in tears, Fidel licked them away, Flo was beckoned in and made a great fuss of as the implications of the reunion dawned on Dot and Elsie. They had done it! They had brought about this final scenario! They were heroines! They were going to be famous and furthermore they would receive the liver cake recipe!

At last their adventure was over. Dot and Elsie, stuffed to the whiskers with liver cake, contemplated the view from the top of Parliament Hill and felt like the mistresses of all they surveyed.

The Heath Harrier

Dot and Elsie Solve Case

By **Reginald Rover**, our roving reporter.

IT WAS revealed today that the case of the mysterious disappearance of London hairy, Fidel, was brought to a conclusion by the sterling efforts of Dot, $4^1/_2$, and Elsie, $4^3/_4$. Dot, a Whippet cross Jack Russell, and Elsie, a Staffordshire bull terrier, took pity on an old lady they met in tears on Bird Bridge, Hampstead Heath, at the sudden disappearance of her Battersea rescue dog Fidel. The two intrepid detectives were tireless in their search for the elusive Fidel. Yesterday their efforts were brought to a successful conclusion when they returned to Bird Bridge with Fidel and his sister Flo.

It transpires that Fidel had in turn been on a mission of his own as he sought the whereabouts of his sister Flo, who it was rumoured had been taken to France. The seekers were led a merry dance as their dog to dog enquiries led them to Gossip, 9, an overweight Labrador, who fed them the misinformation about Flo's abduction to the continental mainland. She will no doubt be eating nothing more than humble pie from now on! Dot and Elsie would like to thank Dogo Argentino and Faye for their generous help in the search.

It is a Happy Ending for all the protagonists as the old lady has adopted Flo and has vowed to keep her and her brother safe for life. Dot and Elsie will be awarded the Dog Detectives of the Year medal as well as a lifetime's supply of liver cake.

Team Dot And Elsie is surely the most powerful alliance since Henry VIII and Catherine of Aragon!

We wish all concerned a productive and successful future.

New Craze in wake of Bird Bridge Case

From our fashion editor, **Fenella Fluff-Taylor**.

IN THE WAKE of the mysterious disappearance at Bird Bridge, the case that was brought to a successful conclusion by Dot and Elsie, a new fashion craze has emerged.

Dogs the length and breadth of the land are sporting a DOT SPOT in an effort to emulate the spot in the centre of Dot's forehead. Dot calls it her third eye and is nonplussed at the popularity of a mark that led to her acquiring her name. Elsie says,

"This is all a ridiculous fuss about a spot that you can't even eat!"

As with all fashion crazes the DOT SPOT does not suit everyone. It is difficult to wear on hairy foreheads without shaving or depilating. The original Dot spot is black and is not therefore the obvious fashion choice for black dogs. An enterprising fashion house has produced the dot in white as well as a range of evening wear in gold, silver and sequinned lace. An economy range is also available from local parlours and online, £10 each dotandelsie.co.uk.

Pictures on following pages:

111

117

LIVER CAKE:
The recipe, at last

1 Acquire LARGE packet of lamb's liver from a
shop that smells really good.

2 Also buy an egg.

3 Have ready some garlic, some flour and some oats.

4 Chop up liver and put in a whizzy machine with the egg,
garlic and maybe a drop of milk to make the mixture gloopier.
Whizz until you have a smooth brown goo.

5 Put goo into a bowl and mix in flour and oats
until it looks like a person cake mix.

6 Empty the lot into a roasting tin and put in a hottish oven.

7 Bake for half an hour making sure that there is a dog available to stand guard.

8 Take out and allow to cool. Ignore drooling dog.

9 Once cool cut into squares.

WARNING: Feed sparingly as feeding frenzy may
result in catastrophic tummy activity*.

P.S. Dot and Elsie feel that this warning is unfair and uncalled for.

SHORT BIBLIOGRAPHY

These are the books I found indispensable for picture references.
All the featured breeds are to be found walking on Hampstead Heath but are
usually in too much of a hurry to draw in situ. With the help of these books
I was able to locate dogs and draw them in my own time.

Barth, Merritt *A Thousand Hounds*, Taschen 2000

Dogs Cube Book, White Star Publishers 2010

Erwitt, Elliot *Dogs*, Phaidon 1998

Flach, Tim *Dogs*, Abrams 2010

Fogle, Bruce *The Encyclopedia of the Dog*, Dorling Kindersley 2000

RECOMMENDED READING

There are many books about training dogs, rescuing dogs and dog stories on the market. These are the ones I found particularly enjoyable and in some cases useful. They are in turn funny, sad, inspiring and, most importantly, full of love for the wonderful beast that is the dog.

Bradshaw, John *In Defence of Dogs*, Allen Lane 2011

Doty, Mark *Dog Years*, Jonathan Cape 2008

Dunbar, Dr. Ian *How to Teach a New Dog Old Tricks*, James & Kenneth 1991

Fischer, John *Think Dog*, Cassel & Co. 2001

Hattersley, Roy *Buster's Diaries*, Little Brown 1998

Horowitz, Alexandra *Inside of a Dog*, Simon & Schuster 2010

Perry, Thomas *Metzgers Dog*, Collins 1984

Powell, Robert, transcribed by *Diary of a Dog. The Life and Times of a Retired Racing Greyhound*, Fieldgard Ltd. 2013. Available from info@fieldguard.com

Rhodes, Dan *Timoleon Vieta Come Home*, Canongate 2003

Rowlands, Mark *The Philosopher and the Wolf*, Granta 2008